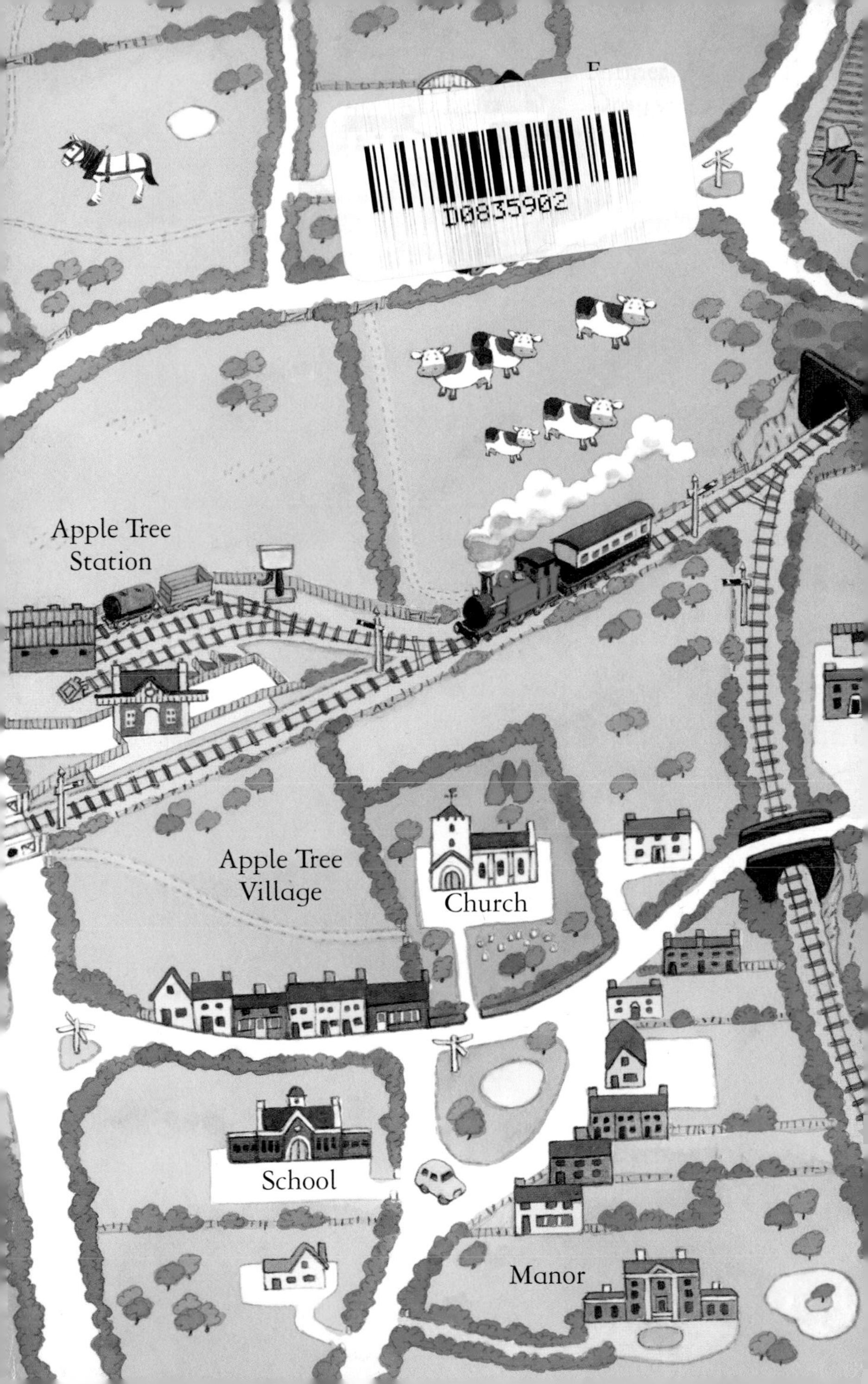
Apple Tree
Station
Apple Tree
Village
Church
School
Manor

Fa[illegible]

Camping Out

Heather Amery

Adapted by Susanna Davidson

Illustrated by Stephen Cartwright

R[illegible]

This story is about
Apple Tree Farm,

Poppy, Sam,

Mrs. Boot
the farmer,

Mr. Boot,

Rusty
the dog,

a tent

and Daisy
the cow.

One day, a car stopped at the farm.

A family got out.

"Please may we camp here?" asked the man.

"Of course," said Mr. Boot.

"Follow us!"

"We'll help you,"
said Poppy.

Sam helped the campers
put up their table.

Mrs. Boot gave them milk and water. Poppy gave them some eggs.

"Dad, can we go camping?" asked Poppy.

"Of course," said Mr. Boot.

Poppy and Sam tried to put up their tent.

At last, the tent stayed up.

After supper, Poppy and Sam went back to their tent.

They crawled inside.

Then they snuggled into their sleeping bags.

What's that noise?
I think there's something big out there.

Poppy took a breath.
She peeked outside.

"Now Daisy's in our tent," cried Sam.

Daisy tried to pull her head back out.

She took the tent with her!

Poppy and Sam
ran home.

Mr. Boot smiled. "Daisy
will be warm tonight."

"What an adventure,"
said Poppy.

"Camping is great!"
said Sam.

PUZZLES

Puzzle 1

Put these pictures in the right order to tell the story.

A.

B.

C.

D.

E.

Puzzle 2

What did the campers bring with them? Match the words to the pictures.

table   chairs   tent   car

Puzzle 3

Can you spot five differences between these two pictures?

Puzzle 4

Choose the right sentence for each picture.

A.

Poppy peeked inside.

Poppy peeked outside.

B.

Mrs. Boot gave them milk.

Mrs. Boot gave them cake.

C.

At last, the train stayed up.
At last, the tent stayed up.

D.

"Follow us!"
"Don't follow us!"

Answers to puzzles

Puzzle 1

1B. 

2C. 

3E. 

4A. 

5D. 

Puzzle 2

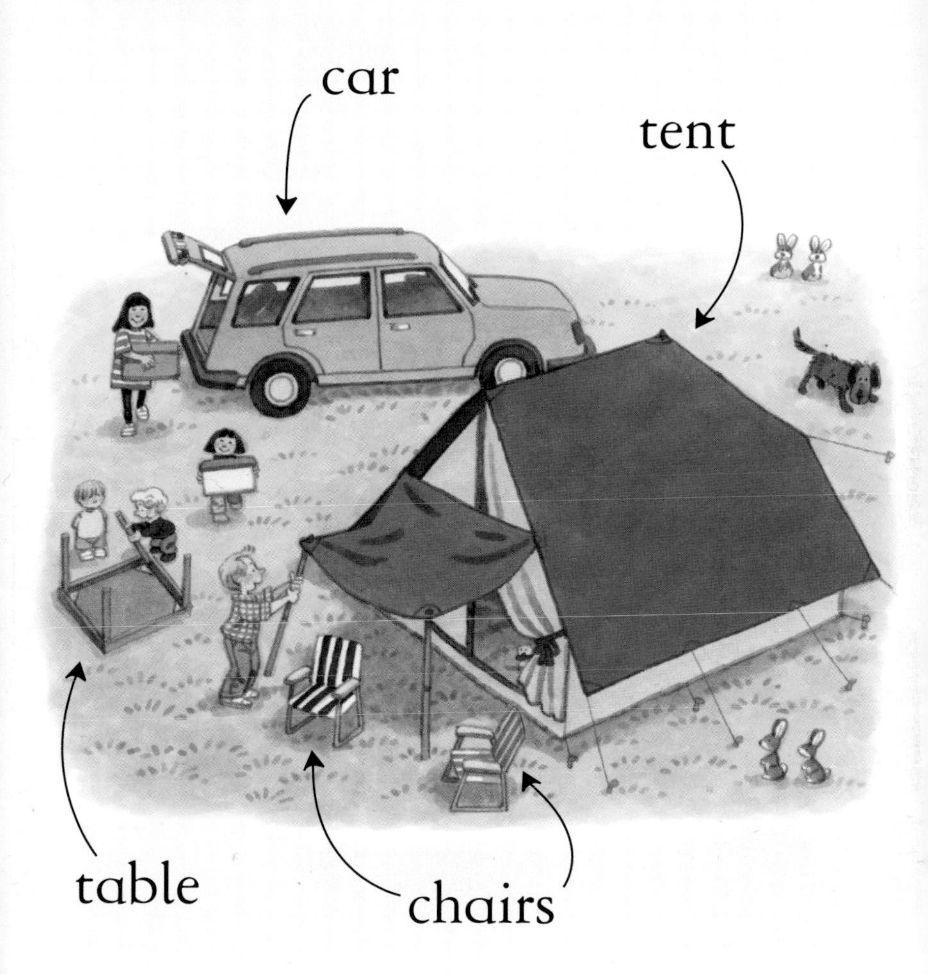

Puzzle 3

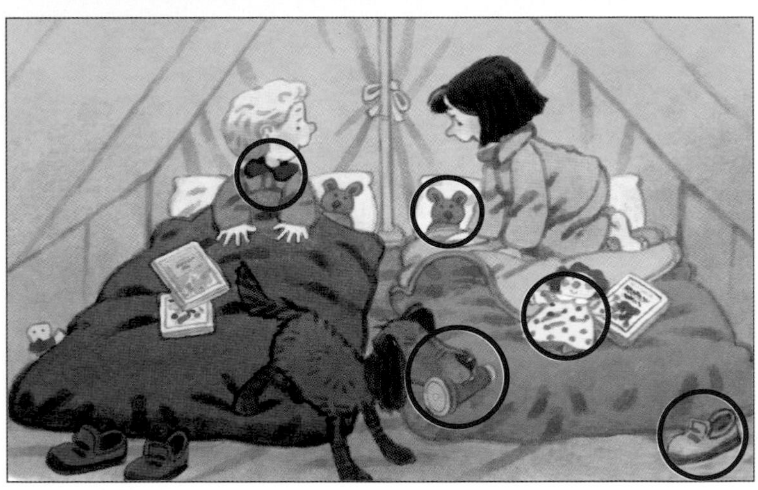

Puzzle 4

A. Poppy peeked outside.

B. Mrs. Boot gave them milk.

C. At last, the tent stayed up.

D. "Follow us!"

Designed by Laura Nelson
Series editor: Lesley Sims
Series designer: Russell Punter
Digital manipulation by Nick Wakeford

This edition first published in 2016 by Usborne Publishing Ltd., Usborne House, 83-85 Saffron Hill, London EC1N 8RT, England. www.usborne.com

USBORNE FIRST READING
Level Two

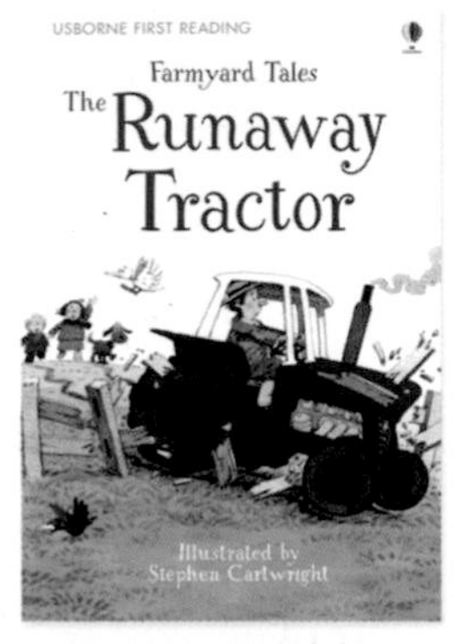

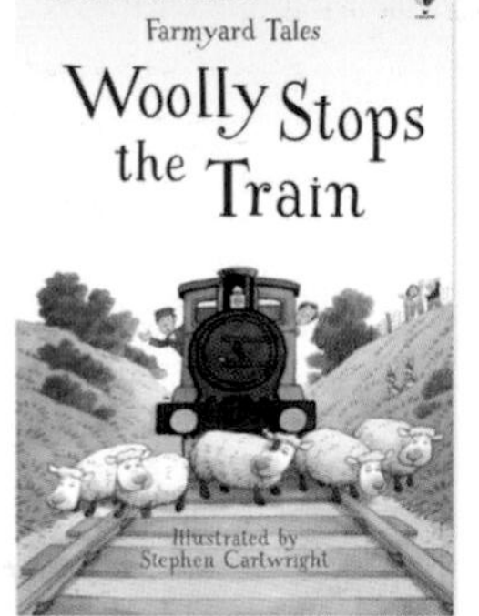